Mummy
An Egg!

Babette Cole

Mini Treasures
RED FOX

"Right," said mum and dad.
"We think it's time we told you

how babies are made."

"OK," we said.

"Girl babies are made from sugar and spice and all things nice," said mum.

"Boy babies are made from slugs and snails and puppy dogs' tails," said dad.

"Some babies are delivered
by dinosaurs."

"You can make them out of
gingerbread," said mum.

"Sometimes you just find them
under stones," said dad.

"You can grow them from seeds in pots

in the greenhouse," said mum.

"Or just squidge them out of tubes."

"Mummy laid an egg on the sofa,"
said dad. "It...

...exploded.

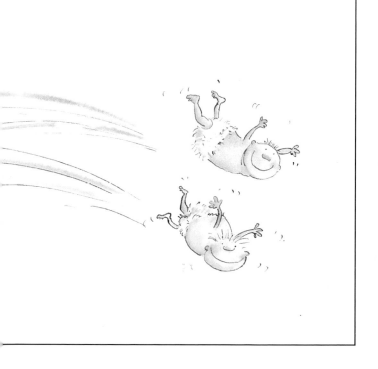

And you shot out."

"What a load of rubbish," we laughed.
"But you were nearly right about the
SEEDS, the TUBE and the EGG."

"We don't think you know how babies are really made. So we're doing some drawings to show you."

"Mummy does have eggs.
They are inside her tummy."

"And daddy has seeds in seed pods
outside his body."

"Daddy also has a tube. The seeds from the pods come out of it."

here

"The tube goes into mummy's tummy through a little hole. Then the seeds swim inside using their tails."

"Here are some ways

mummies and daddies fit together."

"When the seeds are inside mummy's tummy they start The Great Egg Race."

"The winner gets the egg and it starts
to grow into a very small baby."

"The baby gets bigger
and Bigger and BIGGER.

Mummy gets fatter
and Fatter and FATTER."

"When it's ready, out pops the baby."

"So now YOU know...

...and so does everyone else!"

A RED FOX BOOK : 978 0 099 40785 0

First published in Great Britain by Jonathan Cape Ltd 1993
Red Fox Mini Treasures edition published 2000

14 15 13

Copyright © Babette Cole 1993

Red Fox Books are published by Random House Children's Publishers UK
61-63 Uxbridge Road, London W5 5SA,
a division of The Random House Group Ltd.

Addresses for companies within The Random House Group Limited can
be found at: www.randomhouse.co.uk/offices.htm

THE RANDOM HOUSE GROUP Limited Reg No. 954009
www.babette – Cole. Com

A CIP catalogue record for this book is available from the British Library.

Printed in China